BABY'S PEEK-A-BOO ALBUM

A Lift-the-Flap Book

By Debra Meryl
Illustrated by True Kelley

Publishers • GROSSET & DUNLAP • *New York*

Text copyright © 1989 by Debra M. Cerbini. Illustrations copyright © 1989 by True Kelley. All rights reserved. Published by Grosset & Dunlap, Inc., a member of The Putnam & Grosset Group, New York. GROSSET & DUNLAP is a trademark of Grosset & Dunlap, Inc. Published simultaneously in Canada. Printed in Singapore. Library of Congress Catalog Card Number: 88-82978 ISBN 0-448-15375-0   I J

Someone wants to play with you.
Open the door, and you'll see who.

What's that lump in baby's bed?
Could it be somebody's head?

Someone's playing hide-and-seek.
Lift the curtain—take a peek.

Someone's hiding in the tub,
Singing loudly, "Rub-a-dub-dub."

Someone's sitting in this chair.
Lift the flap and see who's there.

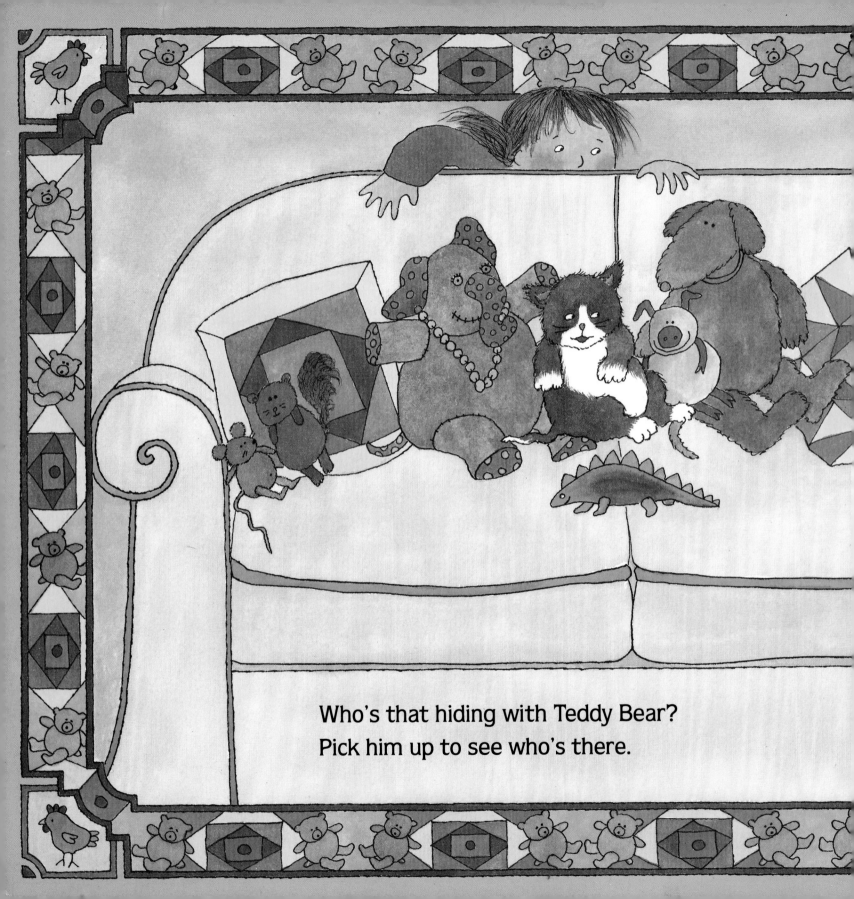

Who's that hiding with Teddy Bear?
Pick him up to see who's there.

Go outside and you might see
Someone there behind that tree.

What's in this box so nicely tied?
Open it up and look inside.

Now who's *this* playing peek-a-boo?
I should have known. Of course, it's you!